THE FRUIT, THE TREE AND THE FLOWER

By Richard Matsuura, PhD.
Ruth Matsuura, M.D.

Illustrated by Linus Chao

Edited by Candice Olcott

ORCHID ISLE PUBLISHING CO.
131 HALAI ST.
HILO, HAWAII 96720

TO THE CHILDREN OF HAWAII

Library of Congress Catalog
Card Number 95-72692

In ancient times, it was the custom in a faraway kingdom to send the old people away after they could no longer work for their food.

In a small farming village in this land, there was a young boy named Alika, who lived with his aging grandfather. Alika loved his gentle and kind grandfather so much that the thought of his being sent away to die made him very sad. So one day, when his grandfather could no longer work, Alika took him to a nearby mountain cave to hide him.

Every night after the village had gone to sleep, he went to the hiding place bringing food and water for his grandfather, and they lived this way for many months.

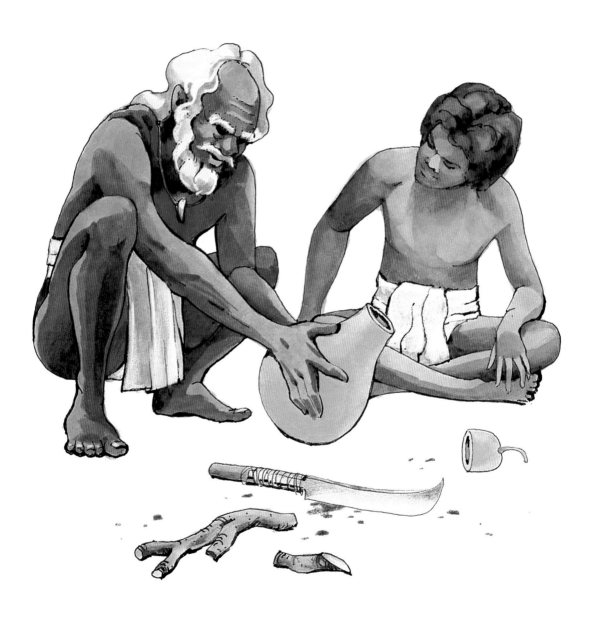

It happened that in this kingdom the King had a Counselor who was famous throughout the land for his wisdom. One day, this wise man fell ill and died. Dozens of noblemen tried to replace him, but none could equal the wisdom and understanding of this great Counselor.

The King was very distressed at not having a wise Counselor and he pondered over the problem. One night, a brilliant idea came to him and he set about preparing a plan.

The following morning, he had his soldiers place a notice throughout the kingdom announcing that if anyone could make the barren lichee tree, which grew in the Royal Garden, bear fruit, he would be the next Counselor to the King.

Many young men came to look at the barren lichee tree, but not one had any idea how to make it fruit. Nearby in the village Alika heard about the notice, and that night when he went to visit his grandfather he told him about the Proclamation. The grandfather said, "I know the answer to the problem."

"You do?" asked Alika excitedly. "How?"

"It is quite simple. Take your knife and 'girdle' the trunk of the tree by removing a strip of bark one inch wide. After you have done this, inform the King that the lichee tree will bear fruit within one year."

The next day Alika did what his grandfather had instructed. The King said, ''If this barren lichee tree does not bear fruit in one year, you shall be put into prison for making me a fool to believe a barren tree can fruit,'' and he dismissed Alika.

As months passed, the King was surprised to see many clusters of flowers on the barren lichee tree, and soon the tree was covered with big bunches of large, bright red fruits. Unlike the tart, hard fruit of other lichee trees, the fruits of this tree were plump, sweet, juicy and had a small seed.

The King brought his wife to see the tree.

When the Queen saw the fruited lichee, she warned the King that if he made this little boy his Counselor, everyone in his kingdom would laugh at both of them.

"Let that boy be given another problem to test his wisdom," demanded the Queen.

The King thought hard and tried to think of a more difficult task.

He summoned Alika and told him to produce two more trees exactly like the one he fruited. The fruits had to be plump, sweet, juicy and with a small seed. If he succeeded, the King told him, he would surely be the next Counselor.

Alika went to his grandfather and told him everything that had happened. Again Alika received instructions from his wise grandfather. He returned to the Palace, and following his instructions girdled a small branch and wrapped the area with a handful of moist moss which he had gathered from the trunk of a tree. He kept the moss in place by wrapping it in cloth and tying it with a string.

The King examined this strange contraption but said nothing.

Alika kept the moss moist for several months. When he saw roots coming out from the moss, he cut the branch below the roots and planted it in a large pot. When the trees fruited, they were the same as the fruit on the mother tree, plump, sweet, juicy and with a small seed.

The Queen was very upset that the boy had succeeded for the second time, and again she warned the King that he would be a fool to make this village boy his Counselor.

Again the Queen demanded, "You must give him a more difficult task."

The King looked at the Queen impatiently and asked, "What would you consider a more difficult problem?"

The Queen gazed into the Royal Garden with a determined look on her face. Slowly a smile crept over her face. She snapped her fingers and said, "I have just the right problem. I would like to see that village boy produce a hibiscus plant with white, red and yellow flowers all on the same plant!"

The King replied, "But that is impossible. There isn't a plant in the kingdom that has even two different colors of flowers."

The Queen smiled and said, "If he is successful in doing this, I will agree to have him as your Counselor."

Alika was again summoned, and was given a hibiscus plant with white flowers on it. The King told him, "I want this plant to have white, red and yellow flowers."

"All three colors on one plant?" asked Alika unbelievingly.

The King hesitated and then nodded slowly.

Alika ran hurriedly to his grandfather. He could hardly wait to tell Grandfather about the new problem the King had given him.

"Grandfather," said Alika breathlessly, "The King has given us a very difficult problem. He wants flowers of three different colors on a single hibiscus plant. Can this be done?"

Grandfather picked up a knife and showed Alika how to graft by cutting a wedge in the white flowered plant and inserting a twig from a yellow flowered plant. He wrapped the area with a moist cloth. Then Alika did the same with a red hibiscus twig. After a year of care and growing, Alika took this grafted hibiscus plant to the King. The King looked at the plant and his eyes nearly popped out. It had white, yellow and red flowers on it! The Queen examined the plant carefully making sure that the flowers were not just tied to the plant to fool the King. Then, discovering the plant was real, a surprised look came to her face.

The King was satisfied and he put his arms around Alika and declared, "You shall be my Counselor."

"No, Your Majesty," replied Alika nervously, "I cannot be your Counselor, because it was my grandfather who gave me all the answers to your problems. I couldn't tell you the truth because I broke a command by hiding my grandfather. Please do not send him away to die," begged Alika.

The King was solemn for a few minutes wondering whether he should punish the boy for breaking a command. He demanded to be taken to the grandfather at once. When they reached the cave, an old white haired man with deep wrinkles on his face hobbled out of the cave, using a walking stick. The King looked at the old man and then raised his hand above his head. As he looked to the heavens, he was silent for a long time.

Then he took a deep breath and proclaimed. ''From this day forth, all the elderly people will be treated with the highest honor and the greatest of respect, for they are truly the wisest in all the kingdom,'' and he smiled at the old man.

The King appointed the grandfather as his Counselor, and with his help he became the wisest king to ever rule the land. The villagers came to respect the old man for his great wisdom, and since that day, all the elderly people were looked upon as wise and they were granted great respect and admiration from everybody in the kingdom.

THE END

ABOUT THE AUTHORS

Richard M. Matsuura, Ph.D.
    Born in Waialua, Oahu, Hawaii
    Graduated from Waialua High School
    Attended Oregon State University, B.S.
    University of Minnesota, Ph.D. in Horticulture
    Attended Bethel Theological Seminary, St. Paul, Minnesota

Ruth M. Matsuura, M.D.
    Born in Hanford, California
    Graduated from Hanford High School
    Attended University of California, Berkeley, B.A.
    University of California School of Medicine, San Francisco, M.D.

Missionaries under United Presbyterian Church, USA to India, 1961-1971

Richard served in the Hawaii State Legislature in the House of Representatives, 1980 to 1984, and the State Senate from 1984 to present.

Ruth is in private pediatric practice from 1971 to present.

Married; six children.

28

ABOUT THE ILLUSTRATOR

LINUS CHAO

Linus is a native of Shantung, North China. In 1955, he graduated from the Fine Arts Department of the National Normal University in Taipei, Taiwan. He studied visual arts in Tokyo, animation art at the University of Southern California and at Walt Disney Studio. He earned a Master of Science degree in art education from Bank Street College and Parsons School of Design in New York City.

Linus has won several international awards and has published many art books. His work has been displayed at several International Art Festivals in Taiwan, China, Brazil, Montreal, San Francisco and Hawaii.

Linus teaches art at the Hawaii Community College. His wife, Jane, is also an outstanding artist. Their paintings hang in museums and private collections in North and South America, Europe and Asia.